SCL
3/16

W9-AGZ-840

THE ORIGINAL
Curious George

THE ORIGINAL
Curious George

H. A. REY

Houghton Mifflin Company

Boston

Introduction

*C*urious George, quintessential childhood tale of monkeyshines and mischief, was the creation of a wartime refugee who knew, better than George himself, what it means to escape danger by the seat of one's pants. A self-taught artist, Hans Augusto Rey (1898–1977) and his Bauhaus-trained wife and collaborator, Margret (1906–1996), were German Jews who married in Brazil in 1935. After founding the first advertising agency in Rio de Janeiro, they returned to Europe in 1936. They lived in Paris until June 14, 1940, leaving just hours before the German army entered the city. Fleeing by bicycle with their winter coats and four picture books strapped to the racks (including the watercolors and a draft of *Curious George* — then called *Fifi*), they crossed the French border into Spain, hopped a train for Lisbon, then sailed to Brazil. There Hans's Brazilian citizenship and the Roosevelt Good Neighbor Policy eased their passage to the United States.

Hans Rey had studied philosophy and natural sciences in school, and he later won acclaim as an amateur astronomer. It was largely by chance that he embarked on a career in children's books. When an editor at the French house of Gallimard expressed delight in some animal drawings he had done for a Paris newspaper, Rey responded by submitting the picture book later published in the United States as *Cecily G. and the 9 Monkeys* (Houghton Mifflin, 1942). The French *Cecily* marked not only Rey's debut but also that of Curious George (who as Sirocco figures as one of the nine monkeys in the story). More books for Gallimard followed; the artist also established a foothold in Britain, where Grace Hogarth, an American employed in London as children's book editor at Chatto & Windus, took an interest in his work. When wartime considerations prompted both Hogarth and the Reys to plan on resettling in the States, the editor asked Hans to promise her the first look at whatever projects he might bring over with him.

When the Reys reached New York in October 1940, Hogarth, now head of Houghton Mifflin's newly formed children's book department, rushed down from Boston to inspect the artist's wares. At canny Margret's insistence, the editor agreed to a then rare four-book contract. Thus it was that in the fall of 1941 Houghton Mifflin published *Curious George* (the new title was the publisher's happy idea) and a lift-the-flap book called *How Do You Get There?* A year later, *Cecily G. and the 9 Monkeys* and *Anybody at Home?* were published. In 1942, Chatto & Windus issued the first British edition of *Curious George,* but under yet another title, *Zozo.* George, after all, was the reigning British monarch; "curious" in the British English of the day meant gay.

Margret, who could be a tenacious negotiator, conducted the couple's business while writing books of her own and contributing substantially to her husband's creative efforts as ad hoc art director and coauthor. Hans appeared to be the gentler of the pair: when *he* roared like a lion, it was always for the amusement of children. Nonetheless,

Rey the artist was a perfectionist. In Paris he had worked closely with the skilled artisans responsible for the printing of his books. To accommodate his wish to do the same in the States, Hogarth chose the New York printer William Glaser, a specialist in fine color work.

Rey may have assumed at first that his original watercolors were destined for reproduction by the same exacting—and costly—photolithographic process favored in Europe. Thrifty American publishers, however, reserved photolithography for picture books assured of a substantial sale; Rey, newly arrived in the United States, was an unknown. Moreover, the manager of the trade department, Lovell Thompson, had concluded that the watercolors for *Curious George* looked "as if the author still planned to point them up . . . and clean them up [in places]." Thompson ruled that a new set of "preseparated" illustrations, based on the watercolors, should instead be prepared.

In essence, to preseparate art was to do by hand and eye the work of the photolithographer's camera. In the camera process, each illustration was photographed under a series of colored filters as the first step in making a corresponding series of metal printer's plates. Eventually, each plate would be used to apply a different colored ink—typically black and the three process colors (magenta, cyan, and yellow)—to the paper as it passed through the press. In the homegrown American alternative method, which had become standard practice during the cost-conscious Depression years, the artist himself, for little or no additional pay, prepared a set of four separate drawings or "separations" for each illustration. Printer's plates were then made from these separations. If all went well, the colors aligned perfectly on the printed page. European publishers spoke disdainfully of the often crude products of this American "folk art."

Whatever Rey's first thoughts on the subject may have been, he quickly adapted to circumstances, and to the more graphic, less painterly aesthetic implicit in the method of reproduction made available to him. In preparing the separations for *Curious George,* he served a whirlwind apprenticeship, during the course of which he transformed a technique foreign to him into a highly personal illustration medium. For readers today, comparing the original watercolors—hat for hat and grin for grin—against their published counterparts not only is intriguing; it also allows a unique glimpse into the pivotal experience in the education, and Americanization, of one of the twentieth century's best-loved picture-book artists.

Curious George appeared to strong reviews on the same Houghton Mifflin list as Holling C. Holling's *Paddle-to-the-Sea* (which far outsold it up to the early 1950s), and in the same season as Robert McCloskey's *Make Way for Ducklings* (Viking), which won the year's Caldecott Medal. The Japanese attack on Pearl Harbor followed later that same fall, and with the United States' entry into World War II came paper rationing and other wartime restrictions that severely limited the potential sale of most children's books. *Curious George*'s fortunes rose with the birthrate during the postwar baby-boom years. As one reviewer predicted, small children did "wear the book out with affection." With time and the publication of six sequels, Rey's spry troublemaker came to occupy a permanent place in our collective imagination, a near neighbor in spirit to Dr. Seuss's Cat in the Hat, Don Freeman's Corduroy, and Maurice Sendak's Max.

For the rest of their busy lives, Hans and Margret Rey, who had no children of their own, worked hard, lived modestly, lent their support to the civil rights movement and other causes in which they believed passionately, and offered encouragement to young artists and writers. The Reys occasionally treated old friends and other favored guests to showings of the original *Curious George* watercolors, the pictures that had launched the couple on the longest leg of their own helterskelter adventures. Five individuals were eventually lucky enough to become the owners of single watercolors from the set: two children of Austin Olney of Houghton Mifflin; one lifelong friend of Hans, Ernest Bettmann; and two collectors, Lee Walp and Lena de Grummond. The rest remained among Margret's prized possessions until her death. With the publication of this new edition of *Curious George,* for which all but one of the original paintings have been reassembled, two unforeseen pleasures now await the rest of us: the first experience of a more poignant and perhaps more private dimension of H. A. Rey's protean artistry and the chance to catch George—imperishable innocent, incorrigible clown—in the act of becoming himself.

—Leonard S. Marcus
Brooklyn, New York

This is George.
He lived in Africa.
He was a good little monkey
and always very curious.

One day George saw a man.

He had on a large yellow straw hat.

The man saw George too.

"What a nice little monkey," he thought.

"I would like to take him home with me."

He put his hat on the ground

and, of course, George was curious.

He came down from the tree

to look at the large yellow hat.

The hat had been on the man's head.
George thought it would be nice
to have it on his own head.
He picked it up and put it on.

The hat covered George's head.
He couldn't see.
The man picked him up quickly
and popped him into a bag.
George was caught.

The man with the big yellow hat
put George into a little boat,
and a sailor rowed them both
across the water to a big ship.
George was sad, but he was still
a little curious.

On the big ship, things began to happen.
The man took off the bag.
George sat on a little stool and the man said,
"George, I am going to take you to a big Zoo
in a big city. You will like it there.
Now run along and play,
but don't get into trouble."
George promised to be good.
But it is easy for little monkeys to forget.

On the deck he found some sea gulls.

He wondered how they could fly.

He was very curious.

Finally he HAD to try.

It looked easy. But—

oh, what happened!
First this—

and then this!

"WHERE IS GEORGE?"
The sailors looked and looked.
At last they saw him
struggling in the water,
and almost all tired out.

"Man overboard!" the sailors cried
as they threw him a lifebelt.
George caught it and held on.
At last he was safe on board.

After that George was more careful
to be a good monkey, until, at last,
the long trip was over.
George said good-bye to the kind sailors,
and he and the man with the yellow hat
walked off the ship on to the shore
and on into the city to the man's house.

After a good meal
and a good pipe
George felt very tired.

He crawled into bed
and fell asleep at once.

The next morning
the man telephoned the Zoo.
George watched him.
He was fascinated.
Then the man went away.

George was curious.
He wanted to telephone, too.
One, two, three, four, five, six, seven.
What fun!

DING-A-LING-A-LING!
GEORGE HAD TELEPHONED
THE FIRE STATION!
The firemen rushed to the telephone.
"Hello! Hello!" they said.
But there was no answer.
Then they looked for the signal
on the big map that showed
where the telephone call had come from.
They didn't know it was GEORGE.
They thought it was a real fire.

HURRY! HURRY! HURRY!
The firemen jumped on to the fire engines
and on to the hook-and-ladders.
Ding-dong-ding-dong.
Everyone out of the way!
Hurry! Hurry! Hurry!

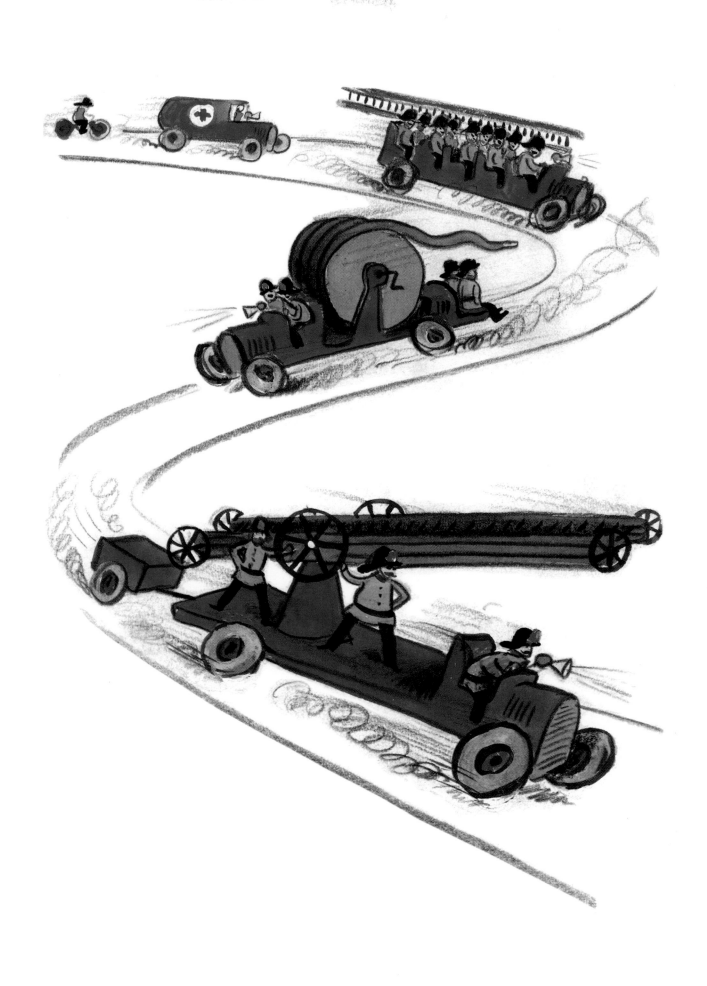

The firemen rushed into the house.
They opened the door.
NO FIRE!
ONLY a naughty little monkey.
"Oh, catch him, catch him," they cried.
George tried to run away.
He almost did, but he got caught
in the telephone wire, and—

a thin fireman caught one arm
and a fat fireman caught the other.
"You fooled the fire department,"
they said. "We will have to shut you up
where you can't do any more harm."
They took him away
and shut him in a prison.

George wanted to get out.

He climbed up to the window
to try the bars.

Just then the watchman came in.

He got on the wooden bed to catch George.

But he was too big and heavy.

The bed tipped up,
the watchman fell over,
and, quick as lightning,
George ran out through the open door.

He hurried through the building
and out on to the roof. And then
he was lucky to be a monkey:
out he walked on to the telephone wires.
Quickly and quietly over the guard's head,
George walked away.
He was free!

Down in the street
outside the prison wall,
stood a balloon man.
A little girl bought a balloon
for her brother.
George watched.
He was curious again.
He felt he MUST have
a bright red balloon.
He reached over and
tried to help himself, but—

instead of one balloon,
the whole bunch broke loose.
In an instant
the wind whisked them all away
and, with them, went George,
holding tight with both hands.

Up, up he sailed, higher and higher.
The houses looked like toy houses
and the people like dolls.
George was frightened.
He held on very tight.

At first the wind blew in great gusts.
Then it quieted.
Finally it stopped blowing altogether.
George was very tired.
Down, down he went—bump,
on to the top of a traffic light.
Everyone was surprised.
The traffic got all mixed up.
George didn't know what to do,
and then he heard someone call,
"GEORGE!"
He looked down and saw his friend,
the man with the big yellow hat!

George was very happy.
The man was happy too.
George slid down the post
and the man with the big yellow hat
put him under his arm.
Then he paid the balloon man
for all the balloons.
And then George and the man
climbed into the car
and at last, away they went

to the ZOO!

What a nice place
for George to live!

Margret and H. A. Rey

Among children, Margret and H. A. Rey were best known as the parents of Curious George, the hero of their most famous books. "I thought you were monkeys too," said a little boy who had been eager to meet them, disappointment written all over his face.

Not all of the Reys' children's books are about George, but they are all about animals. They both loved animals, and one of the first things they would do when they came to a new town was visit the zoo. In Hamburg, Germany, where both were born, H.A. lived close to the famous Hagenbeck Zoo and, as a child, spent much of his free time there. That's where he learned to imitate animal voices. He was proudest of his lion roar, and once he roared for 3,000 children in the Atlanta Civic Auditorium, thus making the headlines in the *Atlanta Constitution* for the first and last time.

Over the years the Reys owned an assortment of animals: monkeys in Brazil, which unfortunately died on a trip to Europe; alligators, chameleons, and newts in New Hampshire; and dogs. They always had a cocker spaniel, and H.A. generally managed to get him into one picture in each of their books.

H.A. also wrote and illustrated two books for adults on astronomy. The books were, in a way, a by-product of the First World War. H.A., as an eighteen-year-old soldier in the German army, carried in his knapsack a pocket book on astronomy, the stars being a handy subject to study in those blacked-out nights. But the book was not much help for the beginning stargazer, and the way the constellations were presented stumped him. So, many years later, still dissatisfied with existing books on the subject, he worked out a new way to show the constellations and ended up doing his own books on astronomy.

H. A. started drawing in 1900, when he was two years old, mostly horses. At that time, one could still see horses all over Hamburg. He went to what in Europe was then called a humanistic gymnasium, a school that teaches Latin in the fourth grade, then Greek, then French, and then English. From this early exposure to five languages, H. A. developed a lasting interest in linguistics. He spoke four languages fluently and had a smattering of half a dozen others.

After school and the First World War, H. A. studied whatever aroused his curiosity—philosophy, medicine, languages—but he never attended art school. To pay the grocery bills while studying, he designed posters for a circus, then drew them directly on stone to make lithographs, an experience that came in handy in later years when he had to do the color separations for his book illustrations.

Margret received a more formal art education. She studied at the Bauhaus in Dessau, the Academy of Art in Düsseldorf, and an art school in Berlin. She even had a one-person show of her watercolors in Berlin in the early 1920s. Then she switched to writing, did newspaper work for a little while, and later became a copywriter in an advertising agency. At one point she wrote jingles in praise of margarine, an experience that left her with an undying hate for commercials. Always restless, Margret switched again to photography, working in a photographic studio in London for a short time, then opening her own studio in Hamburg just when Hitler came into power.

H. A. decided to leave Germany in 1923, when the country's postwar inflation had become so catastrophic that the money he received for a poster one day would not be enough to buy a lunch a week later. He went to Rio de Janeiro, Brazil, and became a business executive in a relative's firm. Among other things, he sold bathtubs up and down the Amazon River. He pursued this rather uncongenial activity until 1935, when Margret showed up in Rio, too.

They had met in Hamburg just before H. A. went to Brazil. As H. A. told the story, he met Margret in her father's house at a party for her older sister, and his first glimpse of her was when she came sliding down the banister.

With Hitler in power, Margret had decided to leave Germany and work as a photographer in Brazil. The first thing she did when she saw H. A. again was to persuade him to leave the business firm. He did, and they started working together as a sort of two-person advertising agency, doing a little of everything: wedding photos, posters, newspaper articles (which Margret wrote and H. A. illustrated), and whole advertising campaigns. Four months later they married. The Reys went to Europe on their honeymoon, roamed about a bit, and finally went to Paris, where they planned to stay for two weeks. They stayed for four years, in the same hotel in Montmartre where they first took lodging. They might have stayed permanently had the Second World War not started.

In Paris the Reys did their first children's book. It came about by accident. When H. A. did a few humorous drawings of a giraffe for a Paris periodical, an editor at the French publishing house Gallimard saw them and called the Reys to ask whether they could make a children's book out of them. They did — *Cecily G. and the Nine Monkeys.* After that they wrote mostly children's books, and it agreed with them. H. A. was always surprised to get paid for what he liked to do best and would do anyway.

In June 1940, on a rainy morning before dawn, only a few hours before the Nazis entered the city, the Reys left Paris on bicycles, with nothing but warm coats and their manuscripts tied to the baggage racks, and started pedaling south. They finally made it to Lisbon by train, having sold their bicycles to customs officials at the French-Spanish border. After a brief interlude in Rio de Janeiro, their migrations came to an end when they saw the Statue of Liberty as they landed in America.

The Reys took a small apartment in Greenwich Village, rolled up their sleeves, and were ready to start from scratch. Before the week was over, they had found a home for *Curious George* at Houghton Mifflin.

H.A. illustrated and Margret wrote, turning her husband's pictures into stories. Margret sometimes wrote her own books, such as *Pretzel* and *Spotty*, and H.A. did the illustrations, at times changing the story a little to fit his pictures. Doing a book was hard work for them and frequently took more than a year. They wrote and rewrote; drew and redrew; fought over the plot, the beginning, the ending, the illustrations.

Ideas came from a variety of sources: an inspiration while soaking in a hot bath-tub; a news item in the paper; a piece of conversation at a party. Once they heard a biochemist tell how, as a boy, he had made a bargain with his mother to give the kitchen floor a thorough scrubbing in order to get money for a chemistry set. So one day, while his parents were out, he sprinkled the contents of a large package of soap flakes on the floor, pulled the garden hose through the window, and turned the water on. In *Curious George Gets a Medal,* George emulates this experiment with spectacular results.

The Reys' books were eventually translated into about a dozen languages, and Margret loved leafing through copies of these foreign editions. It did not matter that she couldn't read some of the languages, such as Finnish and Japanese—she happened to know the story.

Based on Margret Rey's August 1994 essay for
THE COMPLETE ADVENTURES OF CURIOUS GEORGE

Artwork contributed to this volume:
"George finds the yellow hat," page 11, by Dee Jones of the de Grummond Collection;
"George in the ship's cabin," page 19, by Anton Glovsky;
"George tries the telephone," page 35, by Dr. Michael Bettmann, son of Ernest Bettmann;
"George flies with the balloons," page 51, by Lee Walp;
"George in the tree with a balloon," pages 3, 59, by Chris Olney.
Lay-Lee Ong, of the Rey Estate, lent the remaining pieces of artwork.

Leonard S. Marcus acknowledges Lay-Lee Ong, Dee Jones, Dr. Michael Bettmann,
Donna McCarthy, Duncan Todd, and Anita Silvey for their contributions to the Introduction.
Material quoted from Lovell Thompson's memorandum in the Introduction was
printed by permission of the Houghton Library, Harvard University, Cambridge, Massachusetts,
shelf mark bMS Am 1925 (1494).

Introduction copyright © 1998 by Leonard S. Marcus
Illustrations copyright © 1998 by Houghton Mifflin Company
Copyright © 1941 and renewed 1969 by Margret E. Rey
Copyright assigned to Houghton Mifflin Company in 1993
Afterword copyright © 1994 by Margret E. Rey

All rights reserved. For information about permission
to reproduce selections from this book, write to
Permissions, Houghton Mifflin Company, 215 Park Avenue South,
New York, New York 10003.

Library of Congress Cataloging-in-Publication number:
98-71472

ISBN 978-0-395-92272-9
ISBN 0-395-92272-0
Printed in China
SCP 17 16 15 14 13 12 11
4500467250